ALICE IN WONDERLAND

One summer's day, Alice and her kitten
Dinah were sitting in a tree by the river as
Alice's sister read aloud from a history book.

But Alice wasn't listening. She was sleepily dreaming of a world where cats and rabbits wore clothes and lived in little houses. She picked up Dinah and climbed down from the tree.

Just then, a white rabbit came scurrying along. He was clutching a large watch and muttering "I'm late! I'm late!"

"How curious," gasped Alice. "What could a rabbit possibly be late for?— Please!" she cried. "Wait for me."

But the rabbit didn't stop. "I'm late! *I'm late!*" he cried and disappeared into a large hole at the foot of a tree.

Alice was now *very* curious. She squeezed into the dark hole and crawled after him.

Suddenly, Alice found herself falling down, down, down. Luckily, her dress ballooned out and she began floating.

When she landed gently at the bottom,
the White Rabbit was just disappearing
down a hallway and through a tiny door.

"Wait!" cried Alice, chasing after him.
Alice tried the Doorknob.

"Eek!" cried the Doorknob. It spoke!

"I'm looking for the White Rabbit,"
said Alice. "Please let me through."

"Sorry! You're *much* too big," replied the Doorknob. "Try the bottle on the table over there."

Alice saw the bottle labeled DRINK ME, and tasted a little. She tasted a bit more—and began to shrink! Soon she was so tiny, she could fit through the little door.

On the other side of the door, Alice
found herself on the edge of a large forest.
She saw the White Rabbit through the trees
in the distance. She started to run after
him, but suddenly her way was blocked by
two funny little men—Tweedledum and
Tweedledee.

"My name is Alice," she said politely.
"I'm curious to know where the White
Rabbit is going."

The two little men both began talking at
the same time. Alice couldn't understand
what they were saying, so she simply set
off in another direction.

Walking along, Alice heard singing. She turned to see two eyes with a toothy smile.

As she looked more closely, an odd-looking cat with purple stripes appeared.

"I'm Alice—and I'm looking for the White Rabbit," she said. "Which way should I go?"

"I'm the Cheshire Cat," said the odd-looking cat. "And if *I* was looking for a White Rabbit, I'd ask the Mad Hatter or the March Hare. *That* way." He pointed toward a path in the forest—and then vanished!

So Alice followed the path and soon heard the Mad Hatter and the March Hare singing. They were having tea at a big table set with many places.

"We're having an un-birthday party," said the Mad Hatter. "We have only one birthday a year, so there are three hundred and sixty-four *un*-birthdays!"

The March Hare asked Alice where she had come from.

"It all started while I was sitting with Dinah, my cat . . ." Alice began.

"Cat?" said a squeaky voice.
A Dormouse jumped out
of a teapot and ran around
the table.

"Catch him!" called the Hatter.

"No time! I'm late!" cried the
White Rabbit, magically appearing.

"Wait!" shouted Alice.

But the White Rabbit was gone!

Alice was tired of the strange ways of Wonderland. "I'm going home," she said, just as a door in a nearby tree opened.

Stepping through it, Alice found herself in a royal garden. She was amazed to see two playing cards painting white roses with red paint!

And there was the White Rabbit
announcing—the Queen of Hearts! The
Queen walked right up to Alice and said:
"Do you play croquet?"
"Yes, Your Majesty," Alice said.
"Then let the game begin!"

Alice had never seen such a curious croquet game before. The balls were hedgehogs and the mallets were flamingos!

As the Queen was about to take a shot with her flamingo, the Cheshire Cat appeared. The Queen's flamingo panicked. In the confusion, the Queen lost her balance and fell over. She was furious.

"Off with her head!" she yelled at Alice.

"Shouldn't I have a trial first?" Alice said.

And so Alice was put on trial! The Queen sat on the judge's bench. The witnesses against Alice were the March Hare, the Dormouse, and the Mad Hatter.

And then the Cheshire Cat appeared.

"Look, Your Majesty," said Alice. "The Cheshire Cat."

Immediately, the Dormouse
jumped out of his teapot. He ran up
and down the courtroom squeaking.
Everyone chased after him!

The Queen began yelling at Alice. "Off with her—"

But before the Queen could finish, Alice began growing and growing and growing! Everyone was terrified.

"You don't frighten me," said Alice. "You're just a bad-tempered old Queen!"

No sooner had Alice spoken, than she felt herself shrinking again.

"Now, what were you saying, my dear?" asked the Queen.

Alice fled the courtroom.

Alice ran and ran, and was soon lost in
a maze of hedges. She could still hear the
Queen's voice, but it sounded very far
away now—as if in a dream. Wonderland
faded, and she could hear someone calling
her . . . .

"Alice, please wake up! You've been
asleep for a very long time."

Alice rubbed her eyes, and woke up on the riverbank.

"You've been dreaming," her sister said.

"Oh! I've had such an exciting time," Alice replied. "There was a White Rabbit and I followed him and . . ."